A Giant First-Start Reader

This easy reader contains only 54 different words, repeated often to help the young reader develop word recognition and interest in reading.

Basic word list for *Maxie the Mutt*

a	even	not
all	everyone	of
am	Fifi	one
and	he	only
are	I	or
ask	if	poodle
asks	in	says
be	is	that
being	kind	then
bit	kinds	there
Boris	know	they
boxer	like	this
but	little	to
Clyde	look	wants
collie	many	were
doesn't	Maxie	what
dog	mutt	would
dogs	no	you

Maxie the Mutt

Written by Sharon Peters

Illustrated by Ben Mahan

Troll Associates

Library of Congress Cataloging in Publication Data

Peters, Sharon.
　Maxie the mutt.

　Summary: A ''mutt'' learns to appreciate the kind
of dog he is.
　[1. Dogs—Fiction]　I. Mahan, Ben, ill.　II. Title.
PZ7.P44183Max　　1988　　[E]　　87-10914
ISBN 0-8167-1087-2 (lib. bdg.)
ISBN 0-8167-1088-0 (pbk.)

Maxie is a mutt.

He is a little bit of this.

He is a little bit of that.

He is not *one* kind of dog.

He is many kinds of dogs—all in one.

But Maxie doesn't like being a mutt.

He wants to be one kind of a dog.

"If only I were a poodle, like Fifi."

"Or a boxer, like Boris."

"Or even a collie, like Clyde."

"Then no one would ask what I am."

ST. ANN'S SCHOOL
Salt Lake City, Utah

"Then everyone would know what I am."

Everyone asks Maxie what
kind of dog he is.

"What *are* you, Maxie?" they ask.

"You are not a poodle," says Fifi.

"You are not a boxer," says Boris.

"And you are not a collie," says Clyde.

Maxie doesn't like being a mutt.

He wants to be one kind of a dog.

"What *am* I?" says Maxie.

"Look. I look a little bit like Fifi."

"And I look a little bit like Boris."

"And I even look a little bit like Clyde."

"I look a little bit like
many kinds of dogs."

"A little bit of poodle.
A little bit of boxer.
A little bit of collie."

"I know what I am!" says Maxie.

"I am a one-of-a-kind dog."

"There is only one dog like I am."